T0199196

AuthorHouse™
1663 Liberty Drive
Bloomington, IN 47403
www.authorhouse.com
Phone: 1 (800) 839-8640

ISBN: 978-1-7283-2744-0 (sc)
ISBN: 978-1-7283-2745-7 (e)

Print information available on the last page.

Published by AuthorHouse 10/22/2019

authorHOUSE®

Dear Prince Barthello

Written by Granny B (Bernice Stewart)
Illustrated by Roberto Gonzalez

This book is dedicated to my three wonderful, loving children, Elizabeth, Crystal, and Josh.

You have taught me a lot about living life with love, purpose, trust and integrity. We have enjoyed many wonderful story times and grand adventures together!! I love that you have learned from my lessons of always being polite and using your manners.

Thanks for your love, support, and encouragement and for always believing in family!

This is a story from a very long time ago.

A beautiful young Princess lived in a
Castle in a warm and sunny land.

She lived with her parents, but was old
enough now to think about marriage.

She longed for a young handsome
Prince to take interest in her.

Then, one warm December day, 12 days

before Christmas, she received a gift.

21 Chateau Lane
Paris, France
December 13, 1871

Dear Prince Barthello;

I was so surprised when the Partridge and
a Pear tree arrived at my castle today.

The tree is very lovely, the pears are ripe and
sweet, and the Partridge sings beautifully.

I have the perfect place to put it.
Thank you, you're so thoughtful!

Love, Princess Beatrice

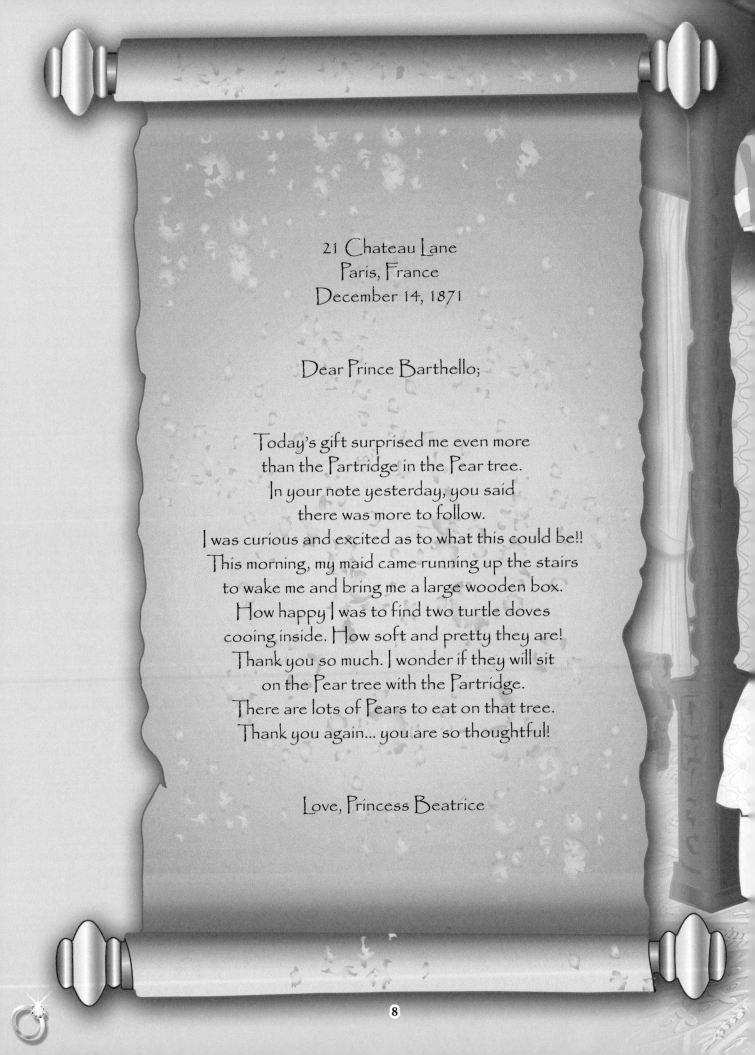

21 Chateau Lane
Paris, France
December 14, 1871

Dear Prince Barthello;

Today's gift surprised me even more
than the Partridge in the Pear tree.
In your note yesterday, you said
there was more to follow.
I was curious and excited as to what this could be!!
This morning, my maid came running up the stairs
to wake me and bring me a large wooden box.
How happy I was to find two turtle doves
cooing inside. How soft and pretty they are!
Thank you so much. I wonder if they will sit
on the Pear tree with the Partridge.
There are lots of Pears to eat on that tree.
Thank you again... you are so thoughtful!

Love, Princess Beatrice

21 Chateau Lane
Paris, France
December 15, 1871

Dear Prince Barthello;

I feel that you like me a lot, as you
are sending me so many gifts!
Today, while I was eating my supper in the Great
Dining Hall, my maid brought in a larger wooden box.
I was so excited! I opened the box slowly, and out
flew three French hens straight up into the air
and then they landed right on the dining table.
Oh how pretty these French hens are!
My Father says they will make a fine feast,
but I said no I want to keep them as pets!

So thank-you again, and how thoughtful of you!

Love, Princess Beatrice

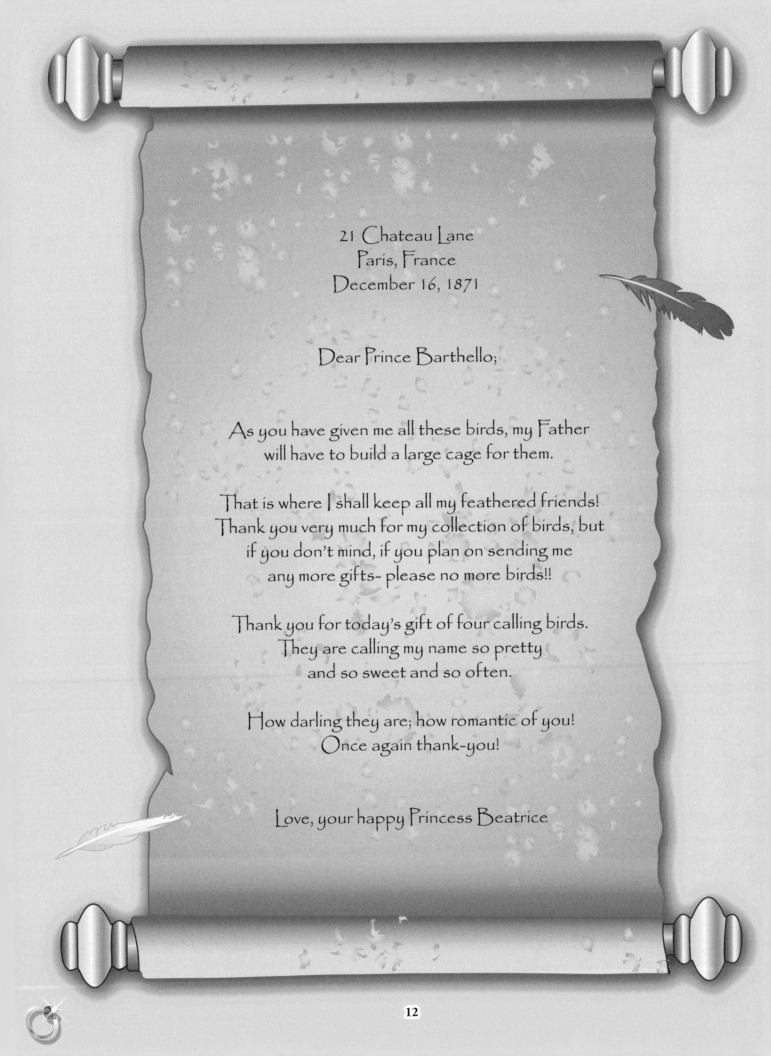

21 Chateau Lane
Paris, France
December 16, 1871

Dear Prince Barthello;

As you have given me all these birds, my Father
will have to build a large cage for them.

That is where I shall keep all my feathered friends!
Thank you very much for my collection of birds, but
if you don't mind, if you plan on sending me
any more gifts- please no more birds!!

Thank you for today's gift of four calling birds.
They are calling my name so pretty
and so sweet and so often.

How darling they are; how romantic of you!
Once again thank-you!

Love, your happy Princess Beatrice

Princess Beatrice

Princess Beatrice

Princess Beatrice

Princess Beatrice

Princess Beatrice

21 Chateau Lane
Paris, France
December 17, 1871

Dear Prince Barthello;

Today while I was being fitted for a new
gown, the mail man rang the bell.
I was so curious and a little nervous
about what he was delivering.
When my maid brought in a small
satin box, I was thrilled!
Oh Barthello you must like me a lot!!
The five golden rings are so beautiful
and fit my fingers perfectly!
This gift is very special to me, and just
so you know, I like you a lot too!

Love, your very happy Princess Beatrice

21 Chateau Lane
Paris, France
December 18, 1871

Dear Prince Barthello;

Birds, birds, birds!! Why so many birds?

Thank you for all your gifts, but please no more birds!!
Today when six geese arrived honking at my
front door, my Mother and Father both asked
"Why is he sending such unusual gifts?"

I do not know. I love the rings, but what
will I do with six more birds?
The six geese are honking loud as they make a nest
on the stairs and are now laying several eggs.
Somehow I must get rid of some of these birds as
I cannot feed them all, and they are so noisy!

My maids are busy enough without having
to clean up after all these birds.
Everyone in the castle is tired of hearing those
calling birds call my name, all the time.

So thank you for the geese and all the eggs, but if you
really do like me, please don't send anymore birds!!

Love, your darling Princess Beatrice

21 Chateau Lane
Paris, France
December 19, 1871

Dear Prince Barthello;

Thank you for the seven beautiful swans! I have
put them in the pond outside of our castle.
They look so pretty when they swim in a row.
I'm so happy for outdoor birds!!
I wasn't so sure what swans eat but I see they like my
Mother's Daisy's that she planted around the pond.
I hope my Mother will not be too angry with me.
Thank you for the nice gifts, but just
what are you trying to tell me?
Barthello please send me a letter telling me how
you feel about me and the reason for all your gifts!
Thank you again, you are very generous.

Love, your curious Princess Beatrice

21 Chateau Lane
Paris, France
December 20, 1871

Dear Prince Barthello;
Thank you for the cows, and for not sending birds!
However, the cows are large and our
barns are already full of horses.
The maids you also sent, want to stay with the
cows so they can milk them all day, but now I have
to find a place for them to sleep in the barn.
We also have a lot of milk now and no one is
sure what to do with it, or where to store it.
But thank you for the thoughtful and unusual gifts.
What are you thinking when you send these gifts to me?
What I really need is a castle of my own for all this stuff!
Please send me a letter stating your intensions!
My Mother and Father wish to know as well.

Love, confused but grateful
Princess Beatrice

21 Chateau Lane
Paris, France
December 21, 1871

Dear Prince Barthello;

I was having tea in the garden today with
Mother and Father when we heard all
this drumming coming up the driveway.
I was not sure if this was a gift as they
arrived unannounced. They just kept
drumming and marching forward. It was
loud and noisy and started to give us a
headache.
My Mother and Father told me to make
them stop, so I put them in the wine cellar.
I am not sure why I need nine drummers
drumming all day, could you please tell me?
Thank you for the gift, but I'm not sure
what your message is? Please send a letter
right away.
By the way, the maids are still milking the
cows and filling every bucket and barrel
they can find.
They will not stop, and the cows are getting
cranky. I just do not know what to do!!

Love, frustrated Princess Beatrice

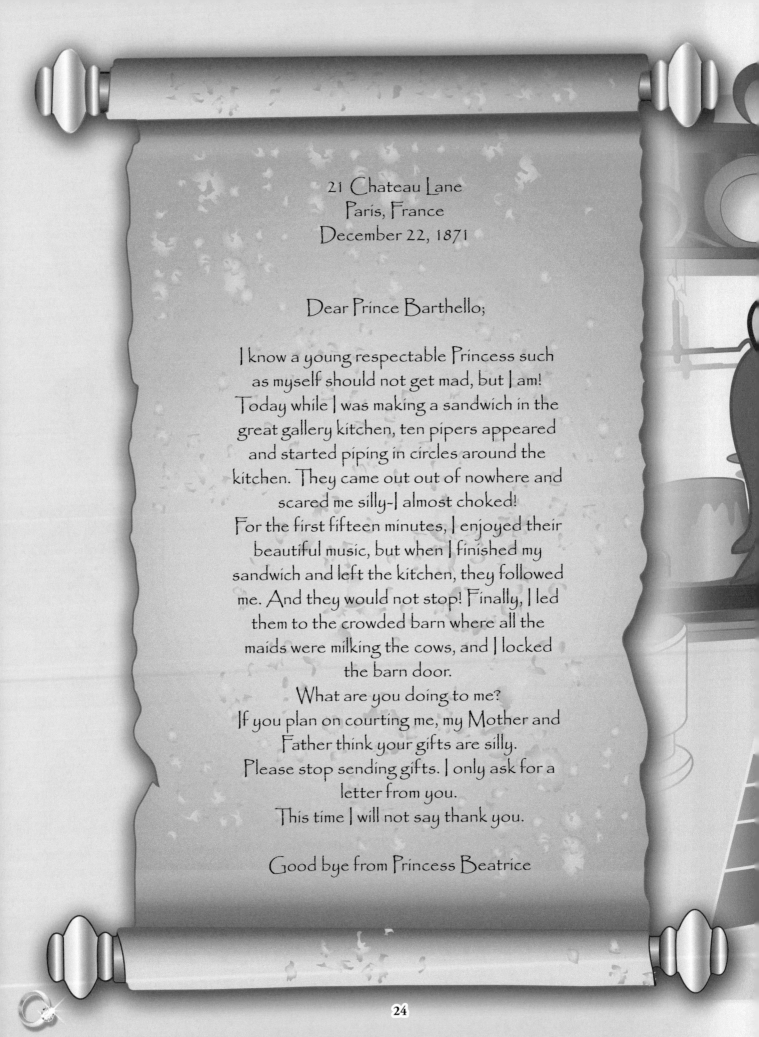

21 Chateau Lane
Paris, France
December 22, 1871

Dear Prince Barthello;

I know a young respectable Princess such
as myself should not get mad, but I am!
Today while I was making a sandwich in the
great gallery kitchen, ten pipers appeared
and started piping in circles around the
kitchen. They came out out of nowhere and
scared me silly—I almost choked!
For the first fifteen minutes, I enjoyed their
beautiful music, but when I finished my
sandwich and left the kitchen, they followed
me. And they would not stop! Finally, I led
them to the crowded barn where all the
maids were milking the cows, and I locked
the barn door.
What are you doing to me?
If you plan on courting me, my Mother and
Father think your gifts are silly.
Please stop sending gifts. I only ask for a
letter from you.
This time I will not say thank you.

Good bye from Princess Beatrice

21 Chateau Lane
Paris, France
December 23, 1871
Dear Prince Barthello;

Today while I was reading, eleven ladies
danced right into the library.
The butler, the cook and my driver, all came
to watch these lovely ladies dance.
The castle is going crazy!
The drummers escaped from the cellar and
now are joining the dancing ladies.
The cows are mooing louder over the pipers piping.
The birds are screeching and fighting with each other.
There is not a peaceful room in the Castle.
The geese are always honking and hissing
when you walk up or down the stairs.
The swans have destroyed all the flowers around
the pond and have started eating the flowers in
the garden. My Mother is very upset about this.
The ladies are dancing all over the
castle and disrupting everyone.
Why would I want ladies dancing, or
the drummers or the pipers?
Why do I need so many cows and milk?
All the birds are noisy, messy and a little scary.
Why are you doing this to me? If you really
like me, than no more gifts please!
Maybe just send more jewelry because I really like my
5 golden rings!

Love, a hopeful Princess Beatrice

21 Chateau Lane
Paris, France
December 24, 1871

Dear Prince Barthello;

Today when I was trying to organize the
chaos in my castle, twelve lords arrived
leaping around the corner and almost
crashed into me.
All the ladies will not stop dancing and
the floors are getting scuffed.
The pipers are piping off key right
outside the castle door, after they
escaped from the barn.
The drummers are so loud that books
are vibrating and falling off the shelves in the library.
The milking maids are getting tired and
sloppy so there is milk all over the barn
floor and the whole barn smells of sour milk!
The swans are now waiting at the door
so they can look for more flowers to eat.
The honking geese have laid so many eggs
that you can hardly get up the stairs.
Many eggs have broken open and baby
geese are waddling everywhere.

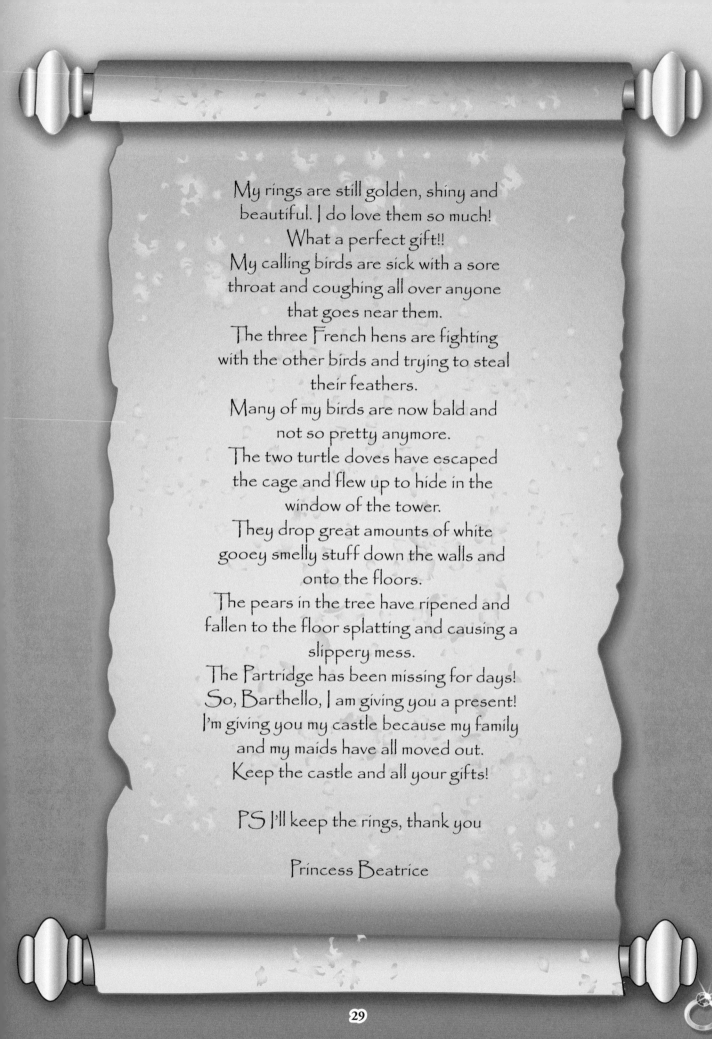

My rings are still golden, shiny and
beautiful. I do love them so much!
What a perfect gift!!
My calling birds are sick with a sore
throat and coughing all over anyone
that goes near them.
The three French hens are fighting
with the other birds and trying to steal
their feathers.
Many of my birds are now bald and
not so pretty anymore.
The two turtle doves have escaped
the cage and flew up to hide in the
window of the tower.
They drop great amounts of white
gooey smelly stuff down the walls and
onto the floors.
The pears in the tree have ripened and
fallen to the floor splatting and causing a
slippery mess.
The Partridge has been missing for days!
So, Barthello, I am giving you a present!
I'm giving you my castle because my family
and my maids have all moved out.
Keep the castle and all your gifts!

PS I'll keep the rings, thank you

Princess Beatrice

Marry Me

Prince Barthello

The End

Printed in the United States
By Bookmasters